Creepy Creatures

Edited By Megan Roberts

First published in Great Britain in 2020 by:

Young Writers
Remus House
Coltsfoot Drive
Peterborough
PE2 9BF
Telephone: 01733 890066
Website: www.youngwriters.co.uk

Printed and bound in the UK by BookPrintingUK
Website: www.bookprintinguk.com
YB0429U

FOREWORD

Hello Reader!

For our latest poetry competition we sent out funky and vibrant worksheets for primary school pupils to fill in and create their very own poem about fiendish fiends and crazy creatures. I got to read them and guess what? They were **roarsome**!

The pupils were able to read our example poems and use the fun-filled free resources to help bring their imaginations to life, and the result is pages **oozing** with exciting poetic tales. From friendly monsters to mean monsters, from bumps in the night to **rip-roaring** adventures, these pupils have excelled themselves, and now have the joy of seeing their work in print!

Here at Young Writers we love nothing more than poetry and creativity. We aim to encourage children to put pen to paper to inspire a love of the written word and explore their own unique worlds of creativity. We'd like to congratulate all of the aspiring authors that have created this book of **monstrous mayhem** and we know that these poems will be enjoyed for years to come. So, dive on in and submerge yourself in all things furry and fearsome (and perhaps check under the bed!).

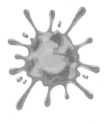

CONTENTS

New Hall Primary & Children's Centre, Sutton Coldfield

Sacha Sibindi (9)	66
Amir Ismail (9)	68
Louise Rowan (9)	69
Kassey Emma Louise Winters-Morton (9)	70
Lillie Taylor (9)	71
Faezah Islam (9)	72
Elena Mouratidou (9)	73
Saffy-Rose Faulkner (9)	74
Ryan Lovett (9)	75
Mollie Howes (9)	76
Elisha Mae Burdett (9)	77
Mayla Taylor (9)	78

Radnor House Sevenoaks School, Sundridge

Max Read (9)	79
Naisha Bahal-Gupta (9)	80
Bella Flavin (8)	83
Toby Proctor (7)	84
Izzy Read (9)	85
Arabella Sweeney (11)	86
Chiara Duranti (8)	87
Eve Dellow (10)	88
Lauren To (8)	89
Adam Kirk (8)	90
Giacomo Duranti (11)	91
Harry Sweeting (7)	92
Oliver N Harwood (9)	93
Paddy Breese (9)	94
Henry Cartwright (10)	95
George Newton (8)	96
Willow Hellicar (7)	97
Marco Edge-McKenna (7)	98
Luca Edge-McKenna (9)	99
Freya Beckerman (10)	100
Jacob Henson (8)	101
Fiona Lu (10)	102
Scarlett Hellicar (9)	103
Sophia Mia Lebraimy (7)	104

Max Baker (8)	105
Sophie Beckerson (10)	106
Georgia Cunningham (9)	107
Alice Lamb (8)	108
James Brian Hatcher (10)	109
Rafe Dellow (8)	110
Lyndon Robert Zaman (8)	111
Ella Rees-Williams (9)	112
Ethan Beau Saunders (8)	113
Neve Beesley (10)	114
Ellie Ford (9)	115
Georgie Sweeting (10)	116
Adriana Meadow Algar (8)	117
Charlotte Gent (8)	118
Belle Prade (9)	119
Oliver Mason (10)	120
Lottie Briant (9)	121
Bow Burnham (8)	122
Joseph O'Connor (9)	123
Charlotte Wilson (8)	124
Sophia Rose Beament (10)	125
James Strother (8)	126
Daisy Thom (8)	127
Sienna Hassan (7)	128
Lizzie Beckerson (7)	129
Austin K Harwood-Bridgen (9)	130
Sully Toms (8)	131
Josh Mclennan (10)	132
James Peregrine Branchflower (10)	133
Isabella May Beament (10)	134
Kate Barden de Leon (9)	135
Alex Davidson (9)	136
Joseph Mullins (8)	137
Aarnesh Chandra (8)	138
Abigail Finch (8)	139
Valentine Edge-McKenna (10)	140
Isabella Woodman (7)	141
Oliver Woodman (8)	142
James Henry John Mason (7)	143

St Mark's CE Primary School, Swanage

Lyla-May Ramsay (7)	144
Jack Surrey (7)	146
James Sloane (7)	148
Olivia Grace Smallman (7)	149
Kacie Carr (7)	150
Reegan Lee Orchard (7)	151
Solomon Ian Brock (7)	152
Bruno Evans (7)	153
Cody Johnston (7)	154

The Japanese School In London, Acton

Nanami Ikeda (8)	155
Amy Notley (9)	156
Aiko Groves (9)	158
Kyo Adachi Mavromichalis (9)	160
Shizuku Maruta (11)	161
Hanano Kamabe (10)	162
Osuke Ueda (10)	163
Masaharu Sugawara (9)	164
Tomoharu Sugawara (9)	165
Julie Marumoto (10)	166
Ryosuke Kikuchi (10)	168
Joseph Duxbury (10)	169
Rikako Saijo (10)	170
Minori Muramatsu (9)	171
Kaede Emma Seki (11)	172
Ray Nestor Ito (9)	173
Serina Niki (10)	174
Hinano Aikawa (11)	175
Kouga Watanabe (10)	176

Thornwood Primary School, Glasgow

Freya Stewart (8)	177
Stefanie Kokkinaki (8)	178
Anna Marie McShane (8)	179
Noorhan Al-Wasity (7)	180
Dalia (8)	181

Cal Hanlon (8)	182
Zoë Rowan Detwiler (8)	183
Mabel Elizabeth Gurney (8)	184
Ghena Alghamdi (8)	185
Navneet Kaur (8)	186
Miraaya Sharma (7)	187
Harsimran Sohal Kaur (7)	188
Matthew Fletcher (8)	189
Eva Sinclair (8)	190
Nampreet Kaur (8)	191
Robbie Sawatzky (7)	192
Ricky Lin (9)	193
Aqsa Ahmad (7)	194
Logan Bradley (7)	195
Ibrahim Nazir (8)	196

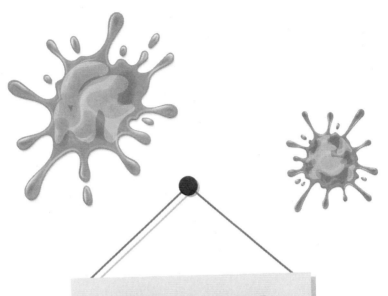

THE POEMS

The Shaper

T he Shaper, a shape-shifter, could change its height

H e liked giving kids a big, scary fright

E ating he did, he would come over and bite

S hape-shifting into paper to get into locked rooms

H e would also destroy a favourite game of kids, Fortnite

A nd he would like to see you during the night

P eople would really hate to see him as a sight

E very night, he would clone himself and give you a fright

R eally, there is no point trying, you will lose a life.

Edward Johnson (10)
Cobden Primary School, Leeds

Cake-Eating Monster

There is a monster
She likes to creep
But when she does
It makes a loud creak
Creak! Creak! Creak!
If you had cake that you left out
The cake monster would find it
And go *gobble! Gobble! Gobble!*
She likes to eat cake and when she is hungry
She has spots of blue
When she is not, they'd turn a lighter blue
And they'd go *pop! Pop! Pop!*
This monster is friendly
As friendly as can be
She looks like a devil with very big hands
That smash things and go *pow! Pow! Pow!*
But the monstrous thing about her are her horns
There is a monster that creeps around
But when it is night, she likes to eat cakes
How do I know this?

Because that monster is me
And I love to eat cakes.

Caryn Leeming (10)
Cobden Primary School, Leeds

Blue

When my monster goes, "Boo!"
She goes blue

My monster's burps are green
Because she just had beans

Sometimes, she had a frown
But she can turn it around

When she's right
Her nose goes white

Her purple, spiky tail
Is as purple as a grape
But she is not a male

She has lunch
And she likes to munch

She has big, green horns
And her bedsheets, she has torn

Her hair is pink
And she likes to wink.

Jasmine Murphy (10)
Cobden Primary School, Leeds

The Fluffball

Once upon a time, the neighbourhood kids
Were playing in the playground
Having fun, messing around
Playing games, joking and laughing
But this is the last time they're going to be
laughing

If you're riding a bike
He'll eat you in a bite

His eyes are that cute that it'll hypnotise you
And don't make him mad, he'll make you sad
Because he's bad
His tummy rumbles like he could eat a jungle
Nobody knows what is going on in his head.

Parna Rostami (10)
Cobden Primary School, Leeds

The Night Monster

He roams through the night
Waiting for children's snores
Make sure he doesn't see you
Or you'll end up trapped between his jaws
His legs are like tree trunks
Stomping down the street
He likes to eat children
To him, they're the perfect treat
So watch out, stay under the covers
Make sure you don't make a peep
He lurks through the night
While the children are asleep.

Lewis Stott (10)
Cobden Primary School, Leeds

Look Away

There was once a monster that stood still all day
It couldn't move, it would just stay
Its skin was as black as the night
It was very heavy, it was not light
Once you looked into its eye
You would transcend up to the sky
So, if you come across the Eye-Catcher
Make sure you don't look, it's a life-snatcher
So take this little poem of advice
Because one day, it may save your life.

Josh McCluskey (11)
Cobden Primary School, Leeds

The Snorer Saurus

The Snorer Saurus snored really loud at night
He smelt like sweets and cake
To make the little children come to him
At night, he would go and listen
At children's windows to see if you snore or not
If you do snore, he will come in your room
And wake you up and say hi
And will give you a doggy present
Then he will eat you up
If you don't snore, the Snorer Saurus will not come.

Ava Rose Connolly (11)
Cobden Primary School, Leeds

Mary Is Here

My monster's name is Mary, she likes to be scary
She is also hairy but she can't eat dairy
Mary is also a fairy
Mary is also flying
She is as fluffy as a little puppy
She'll give you a fright, so don't sleep in the dark night
Make sure you turn on your light to make it bright
Her white teeth will give you a fright
If you turn off your light, she will appear in your sight.

Lucas McKeen (10)
Cobden Primary School, Leeds

My Shadow Monster

He slithered in the dead of night
Waiting for his next victim to appear in sight

His claws are sharp like claws
His eerie laugh in the silence

His menacing stare lit up in his stinking lair

Stealing children's dreams
He is quite the scream

He waits under the bed like the lion
He is getting ready to pounce

This mysterious creature nobody knows!

Sarah-Charlie Jacques (10)
Cobden Primary School, Leeds

My Scary Trap

M y monster likes the taste of eating humans and tearing them up with his teeth

O range monsters are my favourite-coloured monsters

N aughty, spiky, silly, nice monsters

S trong, happy, enormous monsters

T all monsters are also my favourite monsters

E xcited, mean, silly, clumsy monster

R ats are my monster's favourite thing to eat.

Mason Bleasby (10)
Cobden Primary School, Leeds

The Boom

T he spiky, scaly skin as green as the grass
H eart as black as the night sky
E very morning, he growls and wakes me up

B *ang! Boom! Crash!* Every night and day
O ur house is very tidy until he opens everything
O ut in the garden, he is very messy
M y room is neat and tidy until I get home from school.

Shannon Louise Foster (10)
Cobden Primary School, Leeds

The Blind-Sid Creature

B eastly, terrifying creature
L et him take naughty kids and not kind ones
I t was under my wobbly bed
N ever let him sense your fear
D on't look him straight in his four blind eyes

S ensibly, he has none
I t was sensing my fear
D on't let him pick you up at night and never be afraid.

Carina Leigh Harrison (10)
Cobden Primary School, Leeds

Cream Screams

C an't fight
R ejects hugs
E ats children
A monster, I am
M ight be cute on the outside

S ometimes, I am sly
C an I fly? No!
R ed is my favourite colour
E ven the queen is scared of me
A person is yum
M ind my personality
S cared of me yet?

Harrie-Mae Williamson (10)
Cobden Primary School, Leeds

SCP Containment Breach

S tuck in a science lab called SCP

H e's crying as hard as the sea

Y ou see his eyes then your life will come to an end

G od made him but scientists do tests on him

U ntil you see him

Y our life is coming to an end.

Oskar Chmelevskij (10)

Cobden Primary School, Leeds

Despite The Night

Yesterday was good
I flew a kite
But I had a fright
In the night
It was a terrible sight
The teeth were not so bright
I thought it would bite
See, it was good
Despite the night.

Isaac Butterworth (10)
Cobden Primary School, Leeds

My Monster Poem

The monster is hairy
He's so scary
He lurks in the dark
And his friend is Mark
His name is Darren
And he is married to Karen
He likes to eat meats
Under his bedsheets.

Ruby Grace Etheridge (11)
Cobden Primary School, Leeds

My Monster, Frank

F rightening as a bull

R eally ugly

A nd he likes apples

N early as tall as a house

K nows how to scare with a look.

London Rattcliffe (10)
Cobden Primary School, Leeds

Dummy

I can hear the dummy's feet getting closer and
closer each time I breathe in
I can hear the hee hee of the dummy
I know what he looks like because he has lurked in
my box for a long time

I can see the evil grin and the scary eyes of the
dummy
Whatever you do, don't come to Slappyville
I can feel the evilness inside of him
He turns people angry and sad

I can taste him sweating all over me
I can smell his smelly clothes on me
Can I open my eyes yet?
"Mum! Dad!
Help me, please!
'Cause there's a dummy in front of me!"

Joshua Lervy (9)
Gortin Primary School, Gortin

Monster In The Hall

I could hear a creepy and suspicious noise
Coming from the hall
There was a crash and roar
And soon, a sudden fall

I was alert and awake and didn't know what to do
My brother screamed
Suddenly, he was awake too

I could see a shadow pacing back and forth
His hairy and massive claws wrapped round my
doorframe
Then the table toppled and fell

I could feel a sense of fear
Rushing through my veins
My stomach was nervous
And wild with terrible pains

I could taste the dryness in my mouth
As if I needed a drink
I hoped my brother didn't get hurt
I hope, hope, I think

And then
The monster put one step forward
Then I saw his face
I panicked and my heart
Began to race

My brother told the monster, "Get out!"
The monster's eyes went round and red
His jagged body turned purple with rage
He walked cautiously towards the door

He let out a roar
And stumbled out the door!

Leah Campbell (11)
Gortin Primary School, Gortin

Rick From The Attic

I can hear something creepy in the attic
It sounds like it's running frantic
I can see my lightbulb swinging and moving
He must be doing a lot of grooving
I can feel my heart pumping and racing
He is doing a lot of ferocious racing

I can taste my own fear
He must be coming really near
I can smell rotten cabbages
He is drooling green snot
He is very controlling
I know he's coming to eat me

And then a short, spiky, cactus monster
Appears at my door and starts racing around
He is hungry, searching for food
Then I wake up in a sweat
I start to think it's all a dream
But then I see him looking back at me

I'm lying in my bed, freaking out
Then he comes slowly and says,

"Will you be my friend? I am so lonely."
And we lie side by side in my bed
But I'm not sure I want to, he still scares me!

Amber Baxter (10)
Gortin Primary School, Gortin

A Monstrous Fright In The Night

I can hear the floorboards creak
As he creeps up the stairs
I can feel the hairs on my neck
Stand up as he ascends

I can smell his pungent odour
And taste the fear in my veins
And I can see his shadow
As he pauses at my door

The air goes still as he enters
His eyes stare into my back
As he leans on the bedpost, he dents it
My daily nightmare is back

I hear his slithery tongue hissing
With his fangs that puncture your skin
His robot arm clanks and squeaks
His deadly tail starts to spin

I close my eyes and try to pretend
That it's a dream
But when I open my eyes
I can't help it, I just scream

His face is hairy and scarred
Two sharp horns stick out of his head
I close my eyes and scream again
And my parents are running to my bed.

Betha Rickford (10)
Gortin Primary School, Gortin

Tobe From The Wardrobe

I can hear a big growl, it is a strange sound
It's coming from the wardrobe
I can see the wardrobe door creaking open
I can feel something in the wardrobe
Oh, it's something big
It's just some clothes
But I'm sure I felt something
I can taste the excitement in the air
I can smell the scary scent

It appears from under the clothes
He has huge teeth
He is short and fluffy
And his claws are sharp
He is pink and blue and spotty too
He has big feet, but his body is small
I see his antennae appear from his head
He has big eyes
They are gigantic

The monster takes a step closer to me
I scream because I am scared

I wake my sister
I think he is in the kitchen
Then he disappears
And comes back again
We go down and he stomps out the door.

Andrea McConnell (11)
Gortin Primary School, Gortin

A Creepy Sound From The Wardrobe

I can hear a rustling, magical
Scary sound in the wardrobe
I can hear it move and change shape

I can see its shadow
And green, flashing lights
Every time it changes shape

I can taste my mouth drying with fright
The monster's shadow is a great height
I am beginning to feel sick

I can smell its horrible odour
And its stinky breath
Coming closer and closer

I can feel its heavy feet shaking my bedroom floor
Going, *stomp! Stomp! Stomp!*
And it is even closer now

And then the wardrobe opens quickly
A huge, horrible monster comes out
He is green and has horns
I scream as he comes to me
And then, *whoof!* and he disappears.

Emma Orr (10)
Gortin Primary School, Gortin

The Downstairs Horror

I can hear the stairs creak as he comes up the stairs
I can smell something disgusting wafting up the stairs into my bedroom
I can feel a scared feeling bubbling up inside me
I can taste my tongue about to explode with fear
I can see... what? A friendly-looking monster, this is not what I was expecting

Oh, but look, claws are emerging behind his green fur
His eyes have turned bright yellow
And, oh no, antlers are growing out of his head
He is coming closer now, I close my eyes, I wake up
No monster, *phew!* It was only a dream...

Alice Hempton (8)
Gortin Primary School, Gortin

Spotty In The Bath

I can hear something in the bath
I can see a big, fluffy tail
I can feel a hairy giant
I can taste something coming to eat me up
I can smell slime on the floor, it's all the way up
the bath
And, "Boo!" says Spotty the monster. "I will eat
you!"

Suddenly, big, scary eyes are behind the door
I can see a big, fluffy tail
And big, giant horns
I can hear footsteps coming into my room
I pull the blanket over my head and I stay under
my blanket and
Oh, it's just my brother!

Ruby Crawford (9)
Gortin Primary School, Gortin

Jeffy From The Jelly

I can hear the munch of Jeffy having his lunch
I can see that my mum's seen the crumbs
I can feel him about to eat me
Then I jump out of my window into a tree

I can taste his mouth drooling over me
Then he jumps out of the window and starts howling
I can smell his disgusting breath wafting towards me
He looks at me with three eyes

The ground shakes as he stomps
His purple jelly face crumples in a lump
He waves his hairy arms and legs
He's a killing machine, I'm out of there!

Archie Armstrong (10)
Gortin Primary School, Gortin

Rory From The Top Storey

I hear something on the top storey
I see some pieces coming from the roof
I can feel the ground shaking from outside my door
I can taste the fear getting higher
I can smell weird smells like slurry
I can hear something coming down the stairs
It is getting closer, it opens the door
And all I see is two big, green feet
That are the size of two big tree stumps
His body is spiky like the Gruffalo
His arms, round as a pig
He roars and I jump
I tell him to shut up
And he leaves with a jump!

Logan Cooke (9)
Gortin Primary School, Gortin

The Hairy Pretty Monster

I can hear an angry voice and tiny scratches
The monster has made on the floor
I can see a pretty, horned monster
With a crown on its head

I can feel a fluffy body and head
I can taste gooey slime
I can smell chocolate popcorn
And then I see it crawl out of my bed

I see a really scary and hairy, pretty monster
Like the one in my dream
I hide in the dark cupboard behind my nice, warm
bed
Then the monster jumps on me

It's my little sister Lily.

Holly Campbell (8)
Gortin Primary School, Gortin

Sparkle The Monster

I can hear the monster in the wardrobe
I can see the monster eating loads of sweets
I can feel the monster in the bed

I can taste the monster goo falling into my mouth
I can smell the monster's goo inside me
And then I see the monster coming into my
bedroom door

The monster is brown and black
He is very fluffy and furry
He has very big, green eyes
And has very sharp claws.

Kerry McConnell (9)
Gortin Primary School, Gortin

The Hairy Monster

I can hear a rattle in my bath
I can see a spiky-haired creature
I feel his hot breath
And I am worried

I can taste slimy, red goo
And it drops all over the floor
I can smell the monster
And he sneaks through the door

And then, me and the monster make friends
He tells me his name is Darren
Then we play Connect Four
And he walks out the door.

Matthew McGowan (8)
Gortin Primary School, Gortin

The Hairy Sweet

I can see a trail of toffee
I can feel the ground shaking under me
I can taste the dryness in my mouth
Going, *drip! Drop! Drip! Drop!*
Then a hairy sweet appears in front of me
Then it stops and looks around
I stare at it and frown
It falls upon the ground
Mum picks it up and roars, "Go to bed!"
As she throws the monster out the door!

Isabelle Burton (9)
Gortin Primary School, Gortin

The Big Scary Monster

I can hear big footsteps
I can see big claws
I can feel him watching me

I can taste the goo falling on my face
I can smell the breath of him
I can see him in my bedroom
I get out of bed and he goes into the kitchen

He has giant teeth and big horns
His fur is white and orange
He is as big as the roof
He makes big, giant footsteps.

Ella Hayes (8)
Gortin Primary School, Gortin

Mischievous Monsters

If there is a monster sneaking up on you
And you don't know what to do
Then crawl away from it
Or it will munch on you
They may seem lovable at first
But you haven't seen their worst
It'll hide under your bed at night
Waiting to give you an unforgettable fright
As they tend to have a strike here or there
On your bedroom floor, you'll see blood
everywhere
People have a question
How many toes does a monster have?
Well, I'll tell you what, it has more than twelve
If you don't believe me, suit yourself
Next time, you'll have a monster on your shelf.

Muaaz Hussein (9)
Leigh Primary School, Washwood Heath

The Magical Monster

Tiredly, as I went to bed
I thought I felt something go over my head
I turned around and there was nothing there to be found
So when I tried to go back to sleep
I heard a little peep

I got a little scared, so I turned
The other side of the bed
As soon as I did, I saw a colourful, harmless monster
Trying to eat my bread. I was shocked
And gave it a knock on his soft, furry locks

I picked it up and gave it a little cuddle
But then its tummy started to rumble
I didn't care and I put it on my teddy bear's leg
But then, when I did, I saw it disappear
From my bed onto my head
I wondered how it got there and something in my head
Said, "It's over there." I knew it wasn't possible
So I put it in my pet rabbit's cage

And knew that it was a magical, baby monster
So I went back to bed.

Sara-Nur Hussain (8)
Leigh Primary School, Washwood Heath

Clunck Is Under My Bed!

Clunck is under my bed
I can feel his two eyes, red
I can hear his growls, all scary
But his big belly is hairy
I can taste the enthusiasm in me
I can see his sharp claws, three
Then when I check, he's not under my bed

In the kitchen is some fur
Clunck I see, giving some soup a stir
Then he starts to eat
After, he gets a treat
Then he disappears in a flash
I can hear him give the door a slash
And there is Clunck, he's under my bed
After, this is what I said...
"You're my friend forever until I'm dead!"

Aarif Muhammad Buba (8)

Leigh Primary School, Washwood Heath

My Monster

My monster's eyes are as red as rubies glistening
in the sun
His eyes are like burning coal
They're full of fury
His spikes are as sharp as shark's teeth

My monster's body colour is revolting and vile
He smells like garbage that's over 200 days old
He smells like putrid cheese that's out of date
My monster is like a rotten fish

He roars like tremendous explosions
He rattles your bones
His voice booms like thunder
When he whispers, it sounds like nails down a
blackboard.

Andrei Petrat (9)

Leigh Primary School, Washwood Heath

The Monster Who Never Gave Up

Everyone thinks monsters are mean and cruel
But this monster is very friendly
And tries to make friends
But no one wants to be his friend
So he tried his best to make human friends
But sadly, everyone said no
His heart tore apart like it was a piece of paper
This monster never ever gave up
He kept trying and trying
And eventually made a friend called Ted
They were best friends for life
They've always cared for each other
For example
They share their meals
And equal out how much is left.

Mohammed Yusuf Khan (9)
Leigh Primary School, Washwood Heath

Sneaky, Sly Monster

There's a monster in my room
Spotty and dotty like a balloon
I always hear him groaning
I think I might see him very, very soon!

But I actually never see him
Looked day and night
He must be pretty clever
To keep out of my sight

I wonder what he is up to
Time will show the crime
I'm pretty impatient
To see what he has to hide

Come out, little monster
Wherever you are
You may be smart or clever
But you will not hide forever!

Tameema Bibi (10)
Leigh Primary School, Washwood Heath

Night Monster

He walks around in your house, waiting for you to
sleep
Don't get caught or he'll get you in your lovely
dreams
Whilst you're in bed, he'll growl and show off his
jaws
Hopefully, he doesn't scratch you with his pointy
claws
You then get out of your bed and take a look
You find nothing and go for a look
When you come back, you find a trail of your
secret chocolates
Leading out from your window to a deep, dark
cave...

Abdul Moez (9)

Leigh Primary School, Washwood Heath

It!

Pitch-black lightning flashed
Squeak! Squeak!
The stairs began to creak
Red eyes hypnotised me
Blurry images were all I could see
Nails scraped against the wall
As I saw it start to crawl
Trembling with shock and fear
Snorting and grunting was all I could hear
As it began to crawl towards the bed
I heard a voice shouting in my head
The monster had gone back under the bed
Now this was all in my head.

Muhammad Zakariyah (9)
Leigh Primary School, Washwood Heath

My Scaly Purple Monster

My monster has large, round eyes
He has sharp, sparkly teeth
His mouth is dark and wide
He has slimy, scaly skin

My monster has a round, blue nose
His arms are as long as a stick, also thin
My monster has vicious, tree trunk legs
His body is enormous

My monster lives in a dark, gloomy cave
He eats slimy snails and slugs
He walks with large strides
He is enormous like a bouncy castle.

Imaan Hussain (8)
Leigh Primary School, Washwood Heath

Watch Out For Monsters In Case You Get Fooled

M any don't gobble, but do scare children

O nce I met a friendly monster

N ot all are scary, but you're not always sure

S ome may trick you so be careful

T here are real monsters out there

E verything you see is not always true

R idiculous monsters can be fooled so be wise

S earch about monsters so you can be an expert.

Fatima Nisar (9)

Leigh Primary School, Washwood Heath

The Shape-Shifter

A shape-shifter, you may think
Can only turn into random things
Not only that, it can turn into gas
Not even that, it can turn into liquids
Their original figure is quite unfamiliar
A monster with no arms
A monster with no feelings
A monster with no feet
Which you can never beat
Beware, you could be touching, smelling or even
looking at the shape-shifter.

Hammad Ghafoor (9)
Leigh Primary School, Washwood Heath

Scary Mason

M onstrous Mason is devastated
A ppearance is not about him, it is just inside
S o tell this to your friends
O n Halloween and he will never be mean
N ever discriminate, please

Now he is very happy
There is never going to be a mean crowd
And no one is talking about his nappy
You have made him proud.

Alicia Rodrigues (10)
Leigh Primary School, Washwood Heath

Help!

M ighty, hideous, furious

O h, how do I escape from you?

N o peace, no quiet, no silence

S tay away from me, please

T rapped, terrified, petrified

E scaping is not an option

R ealising freedom is far

"S top!" I command. "There is no going back!" it promises.

Malaika Ghafoor (10)

Leigh Primary School, Washwood Heath

Monster?

I crept around to eat
As I sniffed the smell of meat
It talked and talked and talked
So I decided to walk
It was a blue monster
Like the feeling blue
It had a frown
Must be feeling down
Didn't look very mean
Let's scrub it scrubba-dub clean
It's a shape-shifter, flying, fluffy, mechanical
monster!

Laiba Hussain (9)
Leigh Primary School, Washwood Heath

Poetry Monster

M any different creatures walk around
O n a night like tonight
N ot because it's Christmas
S o let's all stop singing Jingle Bells
T his is because it is Halloween
E veryone, beware
R eal monsters walk around
S aying, "Trick or treat!"

Maida Hussain (9)
Leigh Primary School, Washwood Heath

Monster Crunch

Monsters lurking day and night
Coming to get you
So never forget the terrible truth
Or you'll be gone in a second or two
Only if your hopes are high, you might escape
But that's only if your hopes are high
So don't blame me if you end up between
A monster's whiffy jaws. Good luck!

Zahra Hussain (9)
Leigh Primary School, Washwood Heath

Monsters From The Dead

Scary and terrifying
Monsters worry me
I wake up at night
With such a fright
I heard they don't exist

Creepy crawlies up the stairs
Making weird noises
What can it be?
Argh! It's a monster!

Help me!
I'm on my last breath...

Amirah Azar (9)
Leigh Primary School, Washwood Heath

Tiny Monster

M onsters are all around Monster Land
O liver loves making clothes
N illy helps Ella with her bows
S himmer loves to cook every day
T iny loves playing with toys
E lla likes colourful bows
R illa loves to eat food.

Islah Mian (8)

Leigh Primary School, Washwood Heath

Daath

D aath is a fearless creature
A monster like this would want to devour you
A roar he would make if he was hungry
T oo bad, Daath can't eat because everyone is afraid and would run away
H e would love it if you let him devour you.

Eesah Hussain (9)
Leigh Primary School, Washwood Heath

Blue And Purple

M onster, blue and purple

O nly comes at midnight

N ice as pie

S tay up all night? No need

T onight, she is lurking around

E legant, pretty, fluffy and gentle

R eady to give an orphan a better life.

Mariam Asgher (9)

Leigh Primary School, Washwood Heath

Tattle Monster

My monster is called Tattles
He tickles me then I cackle
Tattle does not bite
Nor fight
He lives under my bed
And his fur is red
He has a nice smile
Which I can see from a mile
Tattle is the best
Better than the rest.

Faizan Mohammed (9)
Leigh Primary School, Washwood Heath

Midnight Monster, My Friendly Monster

I have a secret

My friend lives in my wardrobe, but he gets very bored
So he creeps around the neighbourhood
Pinching everything he sees
As it's easy with his six enormous hands
When I go to bed and all of us are sleeping
Midnight Muncher starts
Burping and slurping
And, when he sees me, he wants to feed me
We sit and chat, but I don't understand
As all he says is, "Bleep, blop, bloop!"
But we laugh and giggle and play all night
Until the sun rises high into the sky
And then sadly, Midnight Muncher disappears
Back into my wardrobe once again.

Izzy Stone (8)
Nethersole CE Academy, Polesworth

Hidesy Seek!

Want to play a game?
Maybe hide-and-seek
This is what my monster likes
She never ever peeks
If you see a flash of blue
Or hear a little squeak
You've found my little scaly
Fluffy ball of pure mischief
My monster Hidesy
Is always here in my imagination
On Halloween, she comes to life
The form of my creation
She flies about the twilight sky
She sees the people passing by
She rarely sleeps and loves to play
I see her every single day
Deep, dark pools that hypnotise
Don't look into my monster's eyes
Forever you'll be in a trance
So listen here for one last chance
Stay and play, you'll be okay

If you say no, then run, just go!
My monster comes out, sharp teeth
Jagged claws
She feeds on your fears
And then disappears.

Isla Hentze Hawthorn
Nethersole CE Academy, Polesworth

The Dancing Demon Dog And The Fancy Dress Fairy

This is Kylie, the fancy dress fairy
And Mylie, the dancing demon dog

Kylie likes to wear
T-shirts, jumpers, pants and socks
Trousers, coats and fancy frocks

She's kind and thoughtful and full of joy
She likes to play with her favourite toy
Would you like to play with Kylie
Or be the owner of little Mylie?

Mylie the dancing demon dogs
Mylie eats birds and frogs
And scares away other dogs
Join her on the dance floor
Do you want to play along
Or would you like to sing a song?

Ellie May Drury (9)
Nethersole CE Academy, Polesworth

Spyer The Liar's Ambition

Spyer is a liar that has a big ambition
Which is kinda like a mission
To collect a television
With all his might
He will stand up for his right
By fighting every night
With his great eyesight
His sense of smell works very well
When faced with fear, he never draws a tear
He lives in a cave and you would be very brave
If you came very near
You would face your deepest fear.

Ashleigh May Mahood (9)
Nethersole CE Academy, Polesworth

The Library Monster

One night, I found a creature that changed my life

One very dark night
It was very bright
My curtains started to glow
And I said, "Woah!"

As I was looking
My mum was kissing
My other sibling in bed
I quietly leapt out of bed
And took a step
And in the portal I went
When I came out
It was amazing
There was a library
With a rainbow and Jell-O

Bang! went the books
Then out of nowhere
There stood a monster
It was a cute creature

With pink fur
And a rainbow bow

It looked really friendly
"My name is Wendy!"
Her name was Coco
And there was a brand new book
Called Poco right next to her

So we read it together
So we're best friends forever.

Sacha Sibindi (9)
New Hall Primary & Children's Centre, Sutton Coldfield

My Monster

My monster's eyes are as red as rubies glistening
in the sun
His eyes are like burning coal, they're full of fury
My monster has blood dripping from his razor-
sharp spikes
His spikes are as sharp as scary teeth

My monster's body colour is revolting and vile
He smells like garbage over 200 days old
He smells like putrid cheese that's out of date
My monster is as stinky as rotten fish
My monster roars like a tremendous explosion
He rattles your bones
His voice booms like thunder
When he whispers, it sounds like nails on a
blackboard
My monster is bloodthirsty and as deadly as the
plague
He takes human bodies back to his tenebrous cave
and stores them
He is gruesome and mangy like a mouldy corpse
He is as scary as your worst nightmare.

Amir Ismail (9)
New Hall Primary & Children's Centre, Sutton Coldfield

Bubbles

The hairy, blue spikes come down his back in a
perfect row
The fluffy, cute, naughty monster waits under my
cosy bed
Then he whispers my name, then I think, *oh no!*
Then I hear, "My name is Bubbles, I'm hungry!
Let's go off to the kitchen!"
We went to find whatever
Bubbles found a cake, he's so clever
He is not cute anymore
He's got chocolate all over his face and the floor
"Get back under my bed!" I shouted at Bubbles
The cake is all gone and there is no more
He ran up the stairs and through the door
Then under my bed and started to snore
Oh! He's asleep once more!

Louise Rowan (9)
New Hall Primary & Children's Centre, Sutton Coldfield

Cuthbert The Monster

Cuthbert the monster lives under my stairs
He has big, googly eyes and is covered in hairs

He wears a pink, spotty T-shirt that doesn't cover his belly
And old, tatty socks that are really, really smelly

Cuthbert only comes out at night
So, if you go to the toilet, you may have a fright
He plays in my bedroom with all my toys
And wakes up the neighbours with all his noise
He has cheeky, midnight snakes and makes lots of mess
And dances in the hall in my mom's best dress

He's not a nasty monster, he just wants to play
But, when I wake up in the morning, he sleeps all day.

Kassey Emma Louise Winters-Morton (9)
New Hall Primary & Children's Centre, Sutton Coldfield

The Devil Twins

The devil twins are as evil as can be
You have Spark the sparkly monster on your left
Who is as blue as the sky
On your right, you have Fluff the fluffy monster
Who is as yellow as the dazzling sun

On Halloween night, Spark likes to poke and Fluff
likes to pinch
On Halloween night, their devil forks come out
On Halloween night, they poke and pinch
On Halloween night, the devil twins poke trick or
treating kids
On Halloween night, they pinch kids' delicious
sweets
On Halloween night, many delightful treats, the
devil twins will have a feast!

Lillie Taylor (9)
New Hall Primary & Children's Centre, Sutton Coldfield

Miss Fluffston's Routine

Miss Fluffston has a routine, but not a normal one
Miss Fluffston is a cloud, she is fluffy and speaks very loud
She can lift you in your sleep and put you on a street
Miss Fluffston doesn't make a peep
She flies around the grey, dark street
Maybe she'll say a word or four
But if you're lucky, she'll feed you a worm
She can take you to a world that you've never seen
But make sure you don't speak because she sure likes to eat
That's Miss Fluffston's daily routine, but the question is
Who is she going to eat as a treat?

Faezah Islam (9)
New Hall Primary & Children's Centre, Sutton Coldfield

There's A Monster In My Closet

There's a monster in my closet
Somewhere over there
Hidden in my dirty socks
And in my underwear

It likes to hang around my bed
And crawl into my hair
It likes to eat my sweet lolly
It is just not fair

Now you are behind my curtains
You wait for a minute
Come out you silly monster
I know you came to visit

When the sun rises the next morning
I check under my bed, behind my curtains and in
my hair
Perhaps you are shy
I am tired of you hiding
Please come out to play.

Elena Mouratidou (9)
New Hall Primary & Children's Centre, Sutton Coldfield

Scary Scarlet Swallows Citizens

Scarlet was pretty good and very scary
And she knew a girl called Mary
She tormented Mary every night
And gave the girl a jolly good fright

Scarlet wanders in and out of the house at night
And turns the neighbours pale white
They scream and flee as quick as they can
As Scarlet shape-shifts into a van

She only wanted to go to the shops
To buy some lovely pork chops
"I know that everyone is scared of me
So why not come for some tea?
Yum, yum, hahaha!"

Saffy-Rose Faulkner (9)
New Hall Primary & Children's Centre, Sutton Coldfield

All About Red

R ed like blood

E vil as a bear

D own in the ground he lives

He creeps and creeps until he finds your door
He will break in like a fierce warrior
The next thing you know, he's next to you
When you go to bed, he wakes you up with a scare
He takes you to a secret lair with lots of other monsters
And you have a big, big party.

Ryan Lovett (9)

New Hall Primary & Children's Centre, Sutton Coldfield

Bubbles

He sleeps in a bath
He has a great laugh
I know he's there, but he's shy
He tries to be sly but he's not
Because I see him a lot
He tries to sneak around the house
When it's pitch-black
He eats all my snacks
He runs a bubbly bath so
I guess you already know
My monster is called Bubbles.

Mollie Howes (9)

New Hall Primary & Children's Centre, Sutton Coldfield

Don't Judge A Book By Its Cover

On the streets of the night
This monster came out with all her might
She planned on giving the locals a fright
But the locals thought she was a bright and fluffy
sight
So Frazzle's plan did not work and the cold bite
gave a fright
So Frazzle and the locals went inside
To have hot chocolate and Turkish delight.

Elisha Mae Burdett (9)

New Hall Primary & Children's Centre, Sutton Coldfield

The Queen Angel

She glides through the sky
Passing fluffy, white clouds
Don't make her see you
Or she will gobble you up
Her light blue legs are like feathers
Flying down the sky
She is a carnival
It is a perfect treat
Watch out, be safe
Don't find her
She is dangerous
Sleep well.

Mayla Taylor (9)
New Hall Primary & Children's Centre, Sutton Coldfield

The Monster In The Tree

At the bottom of the garden, in a big tall tree
lives a monster who stares at me
He's often watching day and night
and frequently gives me quite a fright
His eyes are orange like roaring fire,
his fur is twisted like black wire
I often hear him at midnight, snoring,
when morning comes he begins his roaring
He's always hungry, he steals my supper
He especially likes bread and butter
When people heard, they came to see
the mysterious monster that lives in my tree
One brought an axe to fell it down
and kill the monster on the ground
Before he could, I shouted, "Let him be,
leave the monster in the tree!
He may be a monster, he may smell bad,
he may look angry and sometimes be bad
but he's a creature just like me,
so please don't hurt him, he deserves to be free!"

Max Read (9)

Radnor House Sevenoaks School, Sundridge

My Mindfulness Monster

Today, I am riding the crest of a wave
Feeling happiness in every droplet of sploshing water
That touches my face
Anticipating a treat
I am an exuberant puppy wagging its tail
I am like a million rays of sunshine
Awaiting in the sky
I am your yellow, mindfulness monster, Joy

Today, I am as isolated as a child
Perching painfully on the friendship bench in the playground
I feel the sorrow of a Christmas tree
Without a single present underneath it
I am a pool of tears grieving the loss of a loved one
I am your blue, mindfulness monster, Sadness

Today, I am a blazing fire spreading swiftly
And destroying everything in sight
I can feel my skin burning like logs on a bonfire
Snap! Crackle! Pop!

I am an irritated bull, charging
At the sight of a matador holding a red cape
I am your red, mindfulness monster, Anger

Today, I am black like the night
And I hide in the shadows
I am shaking in my boots
And shivering uncontrollably
I feel lumps of coarse coal lining my throat
I am your black, mindfulness monster, Fear

Today, I am a tree waving my hands in the air
Welcoming a change of season
My breath is slow and deep
Ahh, I am at peace
I am a beautiful baby sleeping soundly
In my mother's arms
I am your green, mindfulness monster, Calm

Today, I am a precious, pink rose
On Valentine's Day
I feel like there is a kaleidoscope of butterflies

Lightly fluttering in my tummy
A heatwave is pounding in my heart
I am your pink, mindfulness monster, Love.

Naisha Bahal-Gupta (9)
Radnor House Sevenoaks School, Sundridge

Ogly Bogly Bubbly

The monster's name is Ogly Bogly Bubbly
He is tall and green and some say
He is luminous when he appears in the dark
He looks incredibly slimy as he shines in the
moonlight
Ogly Bogly Bubbly has long, blue, snake-like hair
That is there to scare
He has three ginormous wonky eyes
That wobble when he walks
His nose is flat and bubbles when he's angry
He has one freaky-looking giant tooth
Which you really can't miss
Stumpy arms hang by the side of his body
And two smelly, gigantic feet
That stomp and thump beneath him when he
walks down the street
Ogly Bogly Bubbly doesn't speak
But simply roars, shaking everybody's doors
So if he comes near your street
Remember to use your feet
And run! Run! Run as fast as you can!

Bella Flavin (8)
Radnor House Sevenoaks School, Sundridge

The Jelly Monster And Friends

Jelly Monster is blue and wobbly with bloodshot red eyes.

His bright eyes at night will give you a fright.

With razor-sharp teeth and enormous feet he will make your heart skip a beat.

He lives in a house with a really fat mouse.

When he turns on the telly, his hands stick like jelly.

Jelly Monster enjoys a spot of wrestling when he isn't resting.

His friends are Sunny, Woody and Smelly who are funny, moody and have big bellies.

Sunny Monster is yellow and loves to play the cello.

Woody is brown and acts like a clown.

Smelly is green because he eats lots of beans.

They love to play hockey with their monster friend, Jockey.

Jockey is large and red so he sleeps in a giant double bed

Their friendship is so cool since they left monster school.

Toby Proctor (7)

Radnor House Sevenoaks School, Sundridge

The Pond Monster

In the garden, in the pond
stays a monster where he should belong

He splishes and splashes all day long
scaring the fish to the bottom of the pond

We call him Bob because he bobs around
eating all the frogs on the nearby ground

Bob's mostly green, but looking closely
you will see purple dots spread evenly

Down in the deepest parts of the pond
he plots his plans which are very wrong

You see, Bob is dreaming of the day
he leaves the pond and goes far away

One day, the dreams for Bob come true
someone nets him out of his pond and says,
"Who are you?"

Bob replies with a big, fat grin
"I am your new green and purple best friend!"

Izzy Read (9)
Radnor House Sevenoaks School, Sundridge

Other Side

He appears on your video, as evil memes
Just wait till you fall for his wicked schemes
He's so twisted, he cries red
As he watches you squirm in your bed
The grim reaper plays with your flesh
He treats it like mesh
Once you die, he sends you down to hell
Where the corpses smell
You can never escape or hide
For his friends will find you on the other side
He laughs when you cry
He laughs when you die
The grim reaper's vile
When he shows off his smile
"Let me take you to the other side
Or down in the tide!"
He has a big mouth
For his lair is as hot as the south
You can never escape or hide
For his friends will find you on the other side.

Arabella Sweeney (11)
Radnor House Sevenoaks School, Sundridge

The Horrible Monster Called Dom

Beware, I read on the news that a terrible monster is coming for you
It is unusual but frightening, it has sharp fangs
It has a blood-curdling mouth and it will take off your hand
Its paws are big, *crash! Kaboom!*
It is still coming for you I see
Crash! In my garden, I hide under a table or chair
But it looks for me everywhere
"Argh!" It looks at me, it sees me
I go upstairs, it will take off my hand
I see it's fat as it looks for me
It finds me, catches me, it takes my pen
My handwriting is very messy as it takes my pen
I have to let go, have to put this poem at an end
It gobbles me up and this is the end.

Chiara Duranti (8)
Radnor House Sevenoaks School, Sundridge

The Monster Under The Bed

Under the bed, there lays
A monster as scratchy as hay
At night, he crawls out of his hidey place
And scares the children away
When he walks, all I can see
Is a jelly-like creature staring at me
Most people would find him scary
But I just think he's hairy
As he trails along his sticky pads rip
The yellow, now green carpet, up from it
His horns are a sword
As pointy and sharp as a sword
His teeth are as brown as a board, at least
Only the ones he has left
They sit diagonally just above his
Blue, long snake-like tongue
The only thing I would change about him
Is when he bites my arm off, oh it's so grim!

Eve Dellow (10)

Radnor House Sevenoaks School, Sundridge

Terrifying Tom And The Princess' Prom

There once lived an unstoppable monster called
Terrifying Tom
Imagine Terrifying Tom going to a princess' prom
He was worried, he was as fierce as bears
He had blazing sharp teeth and his feet smelt like
rotten pears
The princesses dreaded him coming because he
had fishy breath
However, one of them loved hairy monsters and
she was called Princess Beth
At the prom, Terrifying Tom waved his spiky tail in
excitement
While Princess Beth gazed at him, thinking about
their engagement
Terrifying Tom was eating his sweets when the
princesses made him disappear
But Princess Beth rescued him and they lived
happily ever after as everyone shed a tear.

Lauren To (8)

Radnor House Sevenoaks School, Sundridge

Jumping Geronimo

When my monster is in a bunch
He sees a person and gives a big punch
When he says 'boo' people go, "Ooh!"
When he is silly, he always becomes chilly
When he makes a jump, he lands with a bump
When he does that, he becomes a bat
He lands with a thud, and there's always a splat of
mud
His trail is slimy, everyone goes "Blimey!"
When there's someone behind him, he always
knows
So when he sees them, off he goes
He jumps like a baby bird, every single person
heard
He's got a lot of goggly eyes, and all of them look
at scrumptious pies
Watch out for Geronimo, especially when he's on
the go!

Adam Kirk (8)
Radnor House Sevenoaks School, Sundridge

Bloody Mary In Your Cabin

Have you ever heard of the ghostly Bloody Mary?
She sits in your cabin until it's too late
The mice are scared of her
The lice are scared of her
The cats are scared of her
And the bats are scared of her
All the animals are scared of her
As the door creaks open
The room is filled with loads of screams
The hand of death is in your reach
As Bloody Mary lands on each
The boys in the cabin were as terrified as a mouse
They wanted to go back to their house
But there was no chance
The next thing the teacher saw were boys flat on the floor
So she roams through the night
Waiting for the next victim.

Giacomo Duranti (11)

Radnor House Sevenoaks School, Sundridge

Vicious Monster

He rises from out of the polluted ocean
Created from plastic and crystal-clear seawater
He rages with anger because of humans
He bursts through the sewers like a rat
Exploding into a toilet
He launches onto the ceiling, sticking like glue
And scans for technology in camouflaged mode
With glee, he taps into the computer
And inserts his sharp, spotty tongue like a cable
into the computer
The multi-virus injection deletes all the games
And programmes whilst his beady mouth
Surrounds the hardware
His tummy squishes and squashes with electricity
And finally demolishes the technology
His job is done.

Harry Sweeting (7)
Radnor House Sevenoaks School, Sundridge

The Angry Monsters Poem

The menacing beast sprang out of the wardrobe
And the children froze in horror
As they looked closer, he was old and hairy
Although that didn't stop him from being naughty
As the old figure stomped towards me
He slipped and touched me and after
He touched the child, she said
"Ew! He has sticky paws!"
I was terrified, he was absolutely disgusting
He was extremely scary, a child screamed
And it broke all the glass in the room
Soon after the child screamed
The monster was raging in anger
He was only a monster that I didn't know
Therefore he was still scary to look at.

Oliver N Harwood (9)
Radnor House Sevenoaks School, Sundridge

Sally From Under The Sofa

They're growling when I sit on my sofa
Especially when it's dark outside
It starts off really quiet, then vibrates on the floor
Then it turns into a loud roar

One day, I decided to look beneath
To see what I could find
Underneath my sofa
Have I lost my mind?

Fear and doubt escaped me and courage held my head
All at once, I saw her sleeping on the ground
Her fur was soft and squishy, her ears pink and bright
Her tail was wrapped around her, out of sight
Then all at once, she woke and smiled right at me
I knew from then on, friends we would always be.

Paddy Breese (9)
Radnor House Sevenoaks School, Sundridge

Hairy Hector

M any may think that monsters are cruel but some are just dumb and stupid

O ne day in his secret cave which was hot, dusty and humid

N aughty little boy once came to visit only to find a hungry, hairy Hector

S cary Hector wasn't all that bad, in fact, he was the opposite, but he didn't know that he wasn't a spectre

T ime had passed and the boy was wearing a woolly coat and looked like a sheep

E ven though he was just a little boy, the monster gobbled him up like a sweet

R emember, never trust a monster, no matter how much it pleases.

Henry Cartwright (10)
Radnor House Sevenoaks School, Sundridge

The Strange Monster Whiff

Pthrrpt is his name, he's from Planet Xxhart
He has a nice heart
Although, he does fart
He eats and eats and eats and eats
His fartiness is mostly sweets
To make him be a bit more quiet
I think he should change his diet
I'd say this, if you agree
He really shouldn't be stinky
He looks like a pig with a fuzzy, pink wig
Which also goes well with his friendly pet, Stig
Stig is a cat who is blacker than black
Because he's well-fed, he's fatter than fat
Although we would just want to go
Pthrrpt is a good friend, you know.

George Newton (8)
Radnor House Sevenoaks School, Sundridge

Monster Poem

Imagine a monster called Fred
Who was emerald and very well fed
He lived under a pink, frilly bed
With a sky-blue dragon called Ned

Imagine a monster called Rose
Who was rosy-red from head to toe
She had a dark, evil, red, big nose
If you touch it, what happens, nobody knows

Imagine a monster called Fred
Who really wanted to wed
Imagine a monster called Rose
Who really wanted to propose

Imagine two monsters who really wanted to wed
Called Rose and Fred
Including Ned from under the bed
So they did wed.

Willow Hellicar (7)
Radnor House Sevenoaks School, Sundridge

Monster Mayhem

M oving through the streets
O ut on his own
N o one there to see
S trange dancing from another zone
T errifying monster, isn't such trouble
E ager to show his dancing, he's not looking for a rumble
R ather find a party

M usic is his passion
A favourite, the Monster Mash
Y ou find him boogying everywhere
H e always makes a crash
E ven when he's happy, he's sad for no one sees
M onster wants to party, will you let him, please?

Marco Edge-McKenna (7)
Radnor House Sevenoaks School, Sundridge

Swamp Monster

S limy, sticky swamp monster slithers around the bog

W aiting for a tasty bite, maybe he'll catch a frog

A waiting a special moment

M aybe, it'll be tonight

P erhaps he's only dreaming, perhaps he might be right

M illing around the marsh

O ver by the reeds

N ever is he lucky

S ometimes only finding seeds

T urning around, he catches a glimpse

E dging closer, his eyes set upon a frog

R eaching out to grab it, he gets eaten by a dog!

Luca Edge-McKenna (9)

Radnor House Sevenoaks School, Sundridge

Sweet Monster

Jelly Snake hair full of venom in the air
We are mesmerised by your chocolate egg,
deadly eyes
Your Oreo face is a big disgrace
Your bubblegum nose is about to explode
A Smarties mouth like a rainbow of blood
Drumstick lolly arms covered in mud
Terry's Chocolate Orange tum cracked into
pieces that come out of your bum
Snicker legs like a melting bar of chocolate
Eton nut mess
Your Cadbury Flake feet are a crumbling
defeat
But anyway, Monster, I still find you rather
sweet and such a sickly treat.

Freya Beckerman (10)
Radnor House Sevenoaks School, Sundridge

Super-Puss The Shape-Shifter

He moans through the dark woods
Snatching anyone nearby
Eating people and crunching bones
If you listen closely, you can hear them cry
His body changes shape to whatever he sees
As soon as you see, you'll never believe
One white and red eye gleams out of the trees

So if you see him run and don't look back
Otherwise you'll never breathe again

He could be disguised as a white and black cat
He can smell you from over a mile away
And his large, pointed ears will always hear your
every word!

Jacob Henson (8)
Radnor House Sevenoaks School, Sundridge

Dear David

He slowly crept inside my room
As he started to play with my broom
I stared at him from inside my bed
When I realised he had a missing head
His eyes were as blank as a wall
His feet were as round as a ball
He had a ripped shirt
I thought I would get hurt
His soul was as black as his shoes
But he was very amused
His brain is missing a chunk
As my clock fell, there was a clunk
He started to get out
When outside came a shout
So, if you see him with a knife
I advise you to run for your life.

Fiona Lu (10)
Radnor House Sevenoaks School, Sundridge

My Monster

There's a monster under the floorboards
Of my top floor flat
I hear him every night
Knocking on the wood, *rat-a-tat-tat*

Although I've never seen him in real life
I imagine him like a dragon breathing out fire
He has claws as deadly as a kitchen knife
And a belly the size of a big black tyre

His face is wrinkled like a shrivelled prune
He has razor-sharp teeth that could bite me in two
And although I think he's scary but dim
He's my monster and I'm proud of him.

Scarlett Hellicar (9)

Radnor House Sevenoaks School, Sundridge

Snow Monster

Every day, the snow monster stomps in the village
and freezes everyone
After he froze everyone, he brought them to his
snow home
And gave them to his snow queen
The queen was so happy, she gave the monster a
trophy
Now the snow monster is shining in the snow
His eyes are full of happiness
He is so proud of himself
His fur changed to blue with purple sparkles
A friendly monster he is now
Stomp! Stomp! Stomp! Stomping down the street
He is filling the air with laughter and joy.

Sophia Mia Lebraimy (7)
Radnor House Sevenoaks School, Sundridge

Something In The Dark

Lurking, waiting under the stars
He's very patient
Once, he waited for a decade
Practising his stash
Rubies and emeralds
Dropped by pirates 125 years ago
He's hungry now, he opens a yellow eye
His tentacles uncurl
He creeps out of his lair
And blends in the sand
Looking for food
Hunting and infecting his prey with terrible toxins
Sadly, he didn't make it back to his lair
Sucked into a bigger mouth
Maybe he should have used his nine brains!

Max Baker (8)
Radnor House Sevenoaks School, Sundridge

The Childchaser

Watch out!
The Childchaser is about

Once you hear this description
You won't believe it isn't fiction

It has antlers as hard as a nail
Eight legs and a ringed lemur's tail

A snake's skin
A whale's fin

With a villain's head
It will catch you in your bed

It will chase you at dusk
With elephant tusks

If you don't escape
It will change your shape

So hide today
Or move away!

Sophie Beckerson (10)
Radnor House Sevenoaks School, Sundridge

I Would Never...

If I met a monster, I would never
Try to make it mad
Because it might eat me up
If it was very bad
I would never say good morning
When the day was dawning
I would only say goodnight
In case I got a fright
I would never ask him in for tea
In case he ate me
I would never point a knife
In case I lost my life
I would never pick up icky grime
In case it was its sticky slime
Now you've heard what I wouldn't do
If you met a monster, would you?

Georgia Cunningham (9)
Radnor House Sevenoaks School, Sundridge

Gloop's Day

G loop was purple, Gloop was red,
L ike a lost sock, she lived under the bed.
O bedience was not her way -
O h! She plotted all the day.
P erhaps, she thought, I'll cause a fuss...
'S he twisted round in all the dust,

D ust which flew right up her nose.
A choo! She sneezed from head to toe!
Y es, Gloop was loud and *not* alone,
S he heard, "Bless you," and stayed at home!

Alice Lamb (8)
Radnor House Sevenoaks School, Sundridge

Kevin The Dragon

Piercing eyes but warm and friendly,
Razor-sharp claws but only seen when angry.
Long blades down his spine
Like a Mohican, they are fine.

When he snores, slimy saliva drips from his jaws.
Breath reeks like smoke from a fire,
And sometimes smells pungent, it is dire!
Stay away when he coughs and sneezes,
Otherwise you'll be toasted needless!

Although you haven't met him yet,
Don't worry,
I control him,
He's my pet!

James Brian Hatcher (10)
Radnor House Sevenoaks School, Sundridge

Maximus Decimus

Maximus Decimus is fierce and strong
He smells like blood which has an awful pong
He kills creatures great and small
And is not bothered by short or tall
When he is very hungry, he could eat a whale
Or if he wants a snack, he would just have a snail
When he is very thirsty, he would drink the sea
If he wasn't, he would have some tea
One day, he decided to eat Mount Everest
And so, he tried but, uh-oh!
That was a bit too big and unluckily, he died.

Rafe Dellow (8)
Radnor House Sevenoaks School, Sundridge

Voltron II

Voltron II was a powerful defender of the universe
His horns could summon lightning to the galaxy
He could survive through black holes
And the snakes worshipped him
The eagles feared him because of his wings
He was like a Lord of the Rings
He was stronger than a boa constrictor
And richer than the kings
He lived alone in the clouds with nothing
But himself and snakes
When he walks on the mountains
The planet shakes.

Lyndon Robert Zaman (8)
Radnor House Sevenoaks School, Sundridge

Mean Margaret

M any people have heard
E specially those still young
A black and white monster hides
N earby everyone

M argaret is her name
A nd she is round and mean
R olling quickly on the ground
G iggling but never seen
A t night is when she comes to play
R unning and having fun
E ating all the children's sweets
T errifying everyone.

Ella Rees-Williams (9)

Radnor House Sevenoaks School, Sundridge

The Three-Eyed Monster

He's hairy, he's scary and he can only eat dairy
He's got razor-sharp teeth and his name is Keith
He's tough, he is brave and he lives in a deep, dark cave
His three eyes are green and you wouldn't want to be seen
So, put on your sun cream, remember not to scream

He's spotty, he's naughty and he is nearly forty
His favourite game is hide-and-seek
He might find you at the end of the week.

Ethan Beau Saunders (8)
Radnor House Sevenoaks School, Sundridge

A Surprising Monster

In the deep, dark night
When the moon glowed bright
A menacing creature caught my eye

With malicious claws
And a spiky spine
Scarlet eyes that glowed in the dark
Prowling
Growling
Panting
A mass of matted fur
The colour of autumn leaves
Razor-sharp fangs
Like glinting shards of glass
A long slimy tongue that flicks and flickers
Silent but deadly
In the deep, dark night.

Neve Beesley (10)
Radnor House Sevenoaks School, Sundridge

Monster Family

Lumpy Bump lives in a dump
His pet fish gave him a wish
To turn snakes into lakes
While his mum was doing sums
His dad was getting mad
Then Lumpy Bump's sister cried
"I'm very upset because
Someone destroyed my cup set!"
But that was when she lied
After, he took a look inside a book
For his dinner, he was having stew
That turns you blue and it also gives you the flu!

Ellie Ford (9)
Radnor House Sevenoaks School, Sundridge

Angel From Hell

As Angel twisted and turned from under the bed
A little, sweet child arose from the dead
All creaky and croaky, all slimy and lonely
There's one more thing Angel said
"More, more, more!" he said
"I demand one more!" Angel said
Its old, brown teeth grinned a grin so evil
That Hell itself could not bear
For Angel just needed one more scare
On October 31st, children dare...

Georgie Sweeting (10)
Radnor House Sevenoaks School, Sundridge

The Halloween Night

It was Halloween
I was dressed up as an evil queen
Suddenly, the house went pitch-black
Argh! Something tapped on my back
Argh! I fainted and dropped to the floor
Out of the corner of my eye something dashed out
of the door
Whoosh! It was a huge, scary, smelly
Terrifying, dangerous monster
Is it a shape-shifter?
No, it's a friendly monster named Dash
Who is ever so fast!

Adriana Meadow Algar (8)

Radnor House Sevenoaks School, Sundridge

Under My Bed

There's a monster under my bed
I should be scared I've heard it said
But she is very funny and kind
So I don't want her to be left behind
I'd like to take her to school to play
Although she may not like it and go away
Perhaps my friends would like to see her
Although they might pull out her fur
Now I think I should leave her at home
As I know I can speak to her alone.

Charlotte Gent (8)
Radnor House Sevenoaks School, Sundridge

Big And Fluffy

Peanut is fluffy, gentle and pretty
She always has lived in the city
Peanut tries and likes to be witty
You know she is just like a big, hairy kitty
She is gentle, fluffy and warm
Just like a newborn
People say beware
But I whisper, "Come, come and sit here!"
Peanut is fluffy, gentle and pretty
"Ssh! If you are quiet, you can hear her sing a little ditty."

Belle Prade (9)

Radnor House Sevenoaks School, Sundridge

Familiar Monster

My monster is big and fluffy
He's around six foot four
He likes to eat his toffees
But leaves the wrappers on the floor

He likes a game of golf
It really makes him smile
It drives his wife up the wall
When he leaves his clothes in a pile
My monster is very cuddly
He makes me happy when I'm sad
He cooks a mean risotto
Oh my goodness, it's my dad!

Oliver Mason (10)
Radnor House Sevenoaks School, Sundridge

Slimy Sally

Slimy Sally lives in an alley
Where nobody dares to go
She is stinky and hairy
Like no fairy
And scary, not really
Not a smile wiped off her face
Just because she comes from a different place
She's fluffy and silly
And can be called Millie
But that's okay with her
Brave is every monster
But even though she's furry
Doesn't mean she shaves.

Lottie Briant (9)
Radnor House Sevenoaks School, Sundridge

Monster Mousse

M y menacing monster, Bob, was making a mousse

O ut jumped an octopus in an ostrich suit

N early knocking the mousse all over the cake

S hape-shifting the octopus into a slithery, slimy snake

T he poisonous teeth of the tree snake are ready to slay

E lephant enters and scares the tree snake away

R aspberry cake and mousse all around, hooray!

Bow Burnham (8)

Radnor House Sevenoaks School, Sundridge

Puddles The Friendly Monster

Puddles was a friendly monster
Who loved to sing and dance
He would do it anywhere
If he only had the chance

All the other monsters could scare all night and day
But Puddles was very different
He wouldn't bite
He just wants to play

Everybody needs a Puddles
He simply is the best
He will smother you with cuddles
Until you go to bed to rest.

Joseph O'Connor (9)
Radnor House Sevenoaks School, Sundridge

Monster

Monster Mover, you're very hairy
But you're not so scary

Oh monster, monster,
Come out from under my bed
Before you hit your hairy head

Never, never face your fear
Before the monster reappears

Stop monster, monster don't you dare
Look over there

There's a monster under my bed
With a slight cut on his head.

Charlotte Wilson (8)
Radnor House Sevenoaks School, Sundridge

Horrific, Giant Cat Man

He horns you in bed
When you are dead
This giant monster, you can't see
Lives under your bed, you see
His hairy coat you can feel
Is under your fluffy quilt
His horrific armpit you can smell
In bed, when you're in hell
In the night, you can feel
His giant fangs, ready to kill
Don't run, don't hide
Or he is coming to get you!

Sophia Rose Beament (10)
Radnor House Sevenoaks School, Sundridge

House Monster

This monster lives in a house
And he is chasing a mouse
What he likes to eat
Are pieces of meat
He is very hairy
And he looks quite scary
He has eight legs
That are shaped like pegs
He comes out at night
With a very bright bike
He is easily seen
Because he is bright green
But don't turn into goo
Because he won't eat you!

James Strother (8)
Radnor House Sevenoaks School, Sundridge

The Hairy, Scary Monster

The hairy, scary monster jumped out of the book
It wasn't very funny, Lucy couldn't look
He was very kind and caring
But then she saw him glaring
"What's the matter?" Lucy said
"I want to go back to my cosy bed."
Then she opened her book
And in the blink of an eye, he fled to his bed
And didn't stop to say goodbye.

Daisy Thom (8)
Radnor House Sevenoaks School, Sundridge

Narry The Nar Monster

Narry the narwhal lives in the sea
He looks very scary but he is very happy
He has a big, magical horn that makes him fly
If he is not happy to eat you, he will chuck you into
the sky
He lives deep down in the bottom of the ocean
And often eats his magic potion
He has a thousand teeth that he keeps in his
pocket
He swims as fast as a super-powered rocket!

Sienna Hassan (7)

Radnor House Sevenoaks School, Sundridge

The Tickle Monster

The tickle monster stomps through the night
It is dark, there is no light

The tickle monster is emerald green
But there's no proof, nobody has seen

He likes to tickle you till you fall
That's what he likes most of all

So stay at home
And don't you moan
For the tickle monster is waiting
To get you all alone.

Lizzie Beckerson (7)
Radnor House Sevenoaks School, Sundridge

Beware!

It was bedtime, it was night-time
But the beast was stirring

The children were dreaming
It was extremely scary

They were dreaming
Of watching the monster

It was an angry, roaring dream
Like a nightmare

The raging heart ripped everything
Like a tsunami

The extraordinary nightmare
Was terrifying.

Austin K Harwood-Bridgen (9)
Radnor House Sevenoaks School, Sundridge

Voldesnort

Vampire teeth, three clawed feet
Club arms
Colossal hands
Stinking feet

Hairy pits, broken heart
Ear on his belly

He lurks in the dark
And he wobbles like jelly

He tries to squeeze through letterboxes
And under creaking doors

He wants to eat your children
So beware of Voldesnort!

Sully Toms (8)
Radnor House Sevenoaks School, Sundridge

Scwizzerars Is Here!

He has no eyes
But he sees you in his mind
Hums and comes
And scares you from behind

Scwizzerars is his name
Scaring is his favourite game

So everybody run
Otherwise you're dumb
He teleports to school
And moves through the walls

Scwizzerars is his name
Scaring is his favourite game.

Josh Mclennan (10)
Radnor House Sevenoaks School, Sundridge

Monster

M onstrous Marvin is the most monstrous of them all

O ne day a week, Marvin would go to a school and scare everyone

N ormally, he would

S ucceed

T o this day, Marvin has been scaring the lives out of everyone

E vil eyes eerily exploring everywhere

R aging Marvin even scared the teacher!

James Peregrine Branchflower (10)

Radnor House Sevenoaks School, Sundridge

Danger David

Banging in the closet, shadows round the walls
Make sure he doesn't see you, this monster's not small
Hide under your covers, he's scarier than you think
Make sure you don't sneak a little peek
His legs are like stones stomping down the street
But if you're extremely lucky, he'll only come once a week.

Isabella May Beament (10)

Radnor House Sevenoaks School, Sundridge

Mighty Mike

Oh dear, oh dear
Here comes Mighty Mike
The worst devil of all
He is cute alright
But when the time comes
You will find his proper soul
Beware, beware, he is on his way
Not far down the street, he says
His eyes are streetlights
Finding his way
Hold tight to your bed cover
I warn you, stay safe.

Kate Barden de Leon (9)
Radnor House Sevenoaks School, Sundridge

Bob The Joker

Bob lived in trees surrounded by fleas
Every time he moved, he sneezed
Bob was slimy and smelt like rotten eggs
And Bob had awfully deadly legs

He was tall and fat and made bad jokes
When Jeff came to the forest to make some mates
Bob told Jeff a joke that was so bad
It made Jeff go completely mad.

Alex Davidson (9)
Radnor House Sevenoaks School, Sundridge

Uka

Uka is a creature
Who comes from the planet Saul
He has two antennae
And he is also very small
He likes to eat fruit
And he lives in a cave
He looks very weird
But he is not very brave
He doesn't speak much
In fact, not at all
It's a very quiet place
On Planet Saul.

Joseph Mullins (8)
Radnor House Sevenoaks School, Sundridge

The Flame Monster

The flame monster loves shooting out water from his big mouth
His big horns are as sharp as thorns
His legs are as thin as pegs
When he goes in the water, he loves to eat lobster
When he goes in the water, he also looks out for children

So parents, tell your daughter not to go in the water.

Aarnesh Chandra (8)
Radnor House Sevenoaks School, Sundridge

The Camping Monster

If you are at a camp
Make sure you take a lamp
Then you will see the monster who likes
marshmallows
He has pink and white freaky eyes
He really doesn't like flies
He wears a vibrant green hat
He is very fat from eating all the marshmallows
His body is blue and his shoes are too!

Abigail Finch (8)

Radnor House Sevenoaks School, Sundridge

Chomping Chilly

C heeky as can be, with eyes as big as me

H ungry as a hound, he will eat you without a sound

I nquisitively, he seeks lamb legs, chihuahua cheeks

L obster claws, alpaca jaws

L ook out, he is somewhere about

Y es, look out, Monster Chilly's about.

Valentine Edge-McKenna (10)
Radnor House Sevenoaks School, Sundridge

The Red Demon

Ten metres in length
All shiny and red
So full of strength
I wish it was dead

It's after me
But I am in bed
What can I do?
I wish it was dead

I shut my eyes
Maybe I'm dreaming
I open my eyes
And then start screaming.

Isabella Woodman (7)
Radnor House Sevenoaks School, Sundridge

Bubble

Bubble, he causes trouble
Every day and every night
He hides in different places
And comes out to take a bite

But I know how to tame him
And stop the nightly fright
I just have to feed him
With pink Turkish delight.

Oliver Woodman (8)
Radnor House Sevenoaks School, Sundridge

My Monster

One day, a monster came to play
But all his hair got in the way
He couldn't play football
He couldn't play hockey
His feet were too big and his hands were too hairy!

James Henry John Mason (7)

Radnor House Sevenoaks School, Sundridge

Spikes The Friendly Monster

Yikes! It's that creepy monster called Spikes
He's the most feared creature of Year Three at
Monster Heights
The kind of meanie little children see when they
turn off the lights
Spikes is furry and fat like a witch's black cat
He has one googly eye and his spiky antennae
stuck up high
School for Spikes was not much fun
Everyone he wanted to be friends with screamed
"Quick! It's a monster! Run!"
In the canteen, at lunchtime
Spikes sat alone, gobbling his slime sandwiches
He couldn't wait to go home

Playtime made Spikes super sad
He wanted to join in with the games so bad
The teachers tried to help but failed
When the rest of the children saw Spikes, they
wailed
Under his fur, his spikes and strange eye

This little monster was as nice as pie
When he opened his mouth, he did not ever try
But the noise that came out made everyone cry
Spikes' loud roar would scare even the biggest
dinosaur
All his classmates needed to do was give Spikes a
chance
Instead of running away at first glance
It does not matter what differences we can see
What matters inside is how kind we can be
If we are scary or small, fat, thin or tall
We are all the same in the end
And even little monsters need friends.

Lyla-May Ramsay (7)

St Mark's CE Primary School, Swanage

A Monster Came To Our House

My mum had tucked me into bed,
One dark and stormy night,
I could hear the wind race past the house,
As she turned off my bedroom light.
I lay there listening in my bed,
When the wind rushed in from outside,
A monster had opened our front door,
I took to my covers to hide.
There was a dreadful noise,
Like no other I'd heard before,
It moaned and screeched and crashed and banged,
From the porch into the hall.
I heard it grunt, I heard it groan,
I had to see this beast,
I saw its shadow from the kitchen light,
It was cooking up a feast.
It was big and bald and grey and old,
And it had an enormous belly,
From the awful whiff that hit my nose,

I knew that it was smelly.
It snuffled around the kitchen,
I saw its shadow on the wall,
Its arms and legs were hairy,
It looked tremendously tall.
Then, as I was watching
The beast, it headed my way,
I raced up the stairs in fright,
Under my bed covers, I would stay.
I heard it whiffling up the stairs,
The moaning noise grew more,
Then it came into my room,
And thumped across the floor.
I held my eyes so tightly shut,
What could it want with me?
Bravely, I peeped to have a look
And I whispered, "Goodnight Daddy!"

Jack Surrey (7)

St Mark's CE Primary School, Swanage

Jerry The Monster

In the dark, gloomy room
Hid a big, scary monster
His hair thick and curly
His nose as red as a ruby
His teeth as sharp as a knife
I stepped inside and used my eyes
To see what lies within
I was frightened at first
A little scared of course
The closer he got, the braver I felt
He wasn't as he seemed
His thick, curly hair was warm and squishy
His teeth were nice and shiny
His eyes were bright and sparkly
We talked and talked for hours and hours
The big, scary monster was not what he seemed
For inside this monster
Lies a heart of gold
Just waiting for someone to see.

James Sloane (7)
St Mark's CE Primary School, Swanage

Spooky Monster

I can hear growls under the bed
I can see orange eyes in my bed
I can feel the excitement bubbling in my spooky
mouth
The growls are getting bigger
I feel the spikes are sticking up in my bed
Oh, I hope the monster's growls don't wake the
children up
Oh, it's waking up, its legs are like tree trunks
The children are running so fast, the monster can't
catch up
The monster is hungry and spotty and spiky
The monster is called Spike and he is very spiky
He likes eating and he is spotty
He's very spooky but he's very nice
And he has his own bed.

Olivia Grace Smallman (7)
St Mark's CE Primary School, Swanage

Sky The Non-Scary Monster

She may not look scary and her name is not Mary.
Sky hides from the other monsters, using her
flower hands.
She pulls the bed covers and hides,
She makes no sound, but she is around.
Not so scary, Sky is not a scary monster
But is a friendly monster.
We can hide in the closet together
Whenever we want.
Sky's hands are flowers
That have some powers.
She may not make a sound
But she'll never be found.

Kacie Carr (7)
St Mark's CE Primary School, Swanage

Hairy Bones

Hairy Bones, Hairy Bones
Is a very scary bones
His hair is red and he said
"Look at the huge ears on my head.
I have funny bones and they are as hard as
stones."

Hairy Bones, Hairy Bones
Is a very scary bones
His breath is so smelly
He has big green wellies
That hide under his huge belly
His fingers are bumpy
Even worse are his toes
And his nose just grows and grows and grows.

Reegan Lee Orchard (7)
St Mark's CE Primary School, Swanage

Fourclawspike's Poem

Happy
Scratchy
Fourclawspike is a scratchy monster
Happy
Scratchy
He's always happy to see me with his spiky, sharp
smile
Happy
Scratchy
He has four fingers and four claws, leaving his
mark on all the doors
Happy
Scratchy
His smile is so big, his teeth rip my socks and my
clothes
Happy
Scratchy
He has a short green tail that wags.

Solomon Ian Brock (7)
St Mark's CE Primary School, Swanage

Sticky Slug-Worth

Slug-Worth is as big as a crane
His teeth are as black as chocolate
And his slime is wet like ice
His antennae are as long as sticks
And his eyes wobble like stones
At night, his slime lurks like cats
His brain was small like crumbs
He was hungry like thunder
But he's still friendly
But beware, he does get hungry.

Bruno Evans (7)
St Mark's CE Primary School, Swanage

Scary Monsters

Fred the scary, terrifying monster started to scare people
Fred the terrifying monster slept in a fiery bed
He had big, scary horns that pointed out of the top of his head
Fred was tall and scary
He went to the gym daily
Fred had big, sharp claws
That scratched the doors
And all day long, Fred roars.

Cody Johnston (7)
St Mark's CE Primary School, Swanage

The Monster

He is as yellow as a corn
Ever since he was born
He is as small as a pencil case
Although he grows when he growls
Like a proud lion who artfully prowls

He likes to eat everything and anything
He always asks you for something
If you don't give him some food
He will eat you up; you are a barbecue

Okay - I will give him a surprising food
Chewing gum will do - it's chewable, you see
Now, the monster is unusually quite calm
So, I want to pet his fluffy, light fur
Oh no, suddenly, that's got him bigger than a
building

His footsteps pound the hard ground
Stomp! Stomp! Stomp! is their sound
Oh my! He is running around the city
Calm down monster, don't run around
Give him food! Feed him and calm him down.

Nanami Ikeda (8)
The Japanese School In London, Acton

The Vam Spy

The Vam monster is creeping up
Beware! It'll catch you in a cup
On Halloween, it'll suck up your treats with a
balloon
When you don't give it treats, it'll put you in the
monster lagoon
It likes to see children's smiley faces
If you're grumpy, it will put you in awkward places

It's the loudest thing you can hear in a day
If you hear Vam making noise, you'll have a big
price to pay
It'll make you pay more if you disturb it while
crossing a lane
To cheer it up, give it a jug filled with fresh candy
canes

Its teeth can bite till it stops strumming its tummy
It chews and chews till it gets the cola-flavoured
gummy
Then it goes off to find places to live, but is sore
Searching for some people to give it corn - what a
bore!

If it finds you being friendly, it will butt you with its horns
You'd better be happy or it will mush you with its corn.

Amy Notley (9)

The Japanese School In London, Acton

The Voodoo Shadow Slider

Its sharp horns reach for the sky
As it slides through the profound darkness
Its eyes are made to petrify
There's nothing like his slyness

It has two snake-like tails
And it has nine arms that sting
It never ever fails
To turn trees into smithereens

Its tongue is split into six
Which is blotchy and eerily blue
It makes a magical mix
That includes your soul and green goo

It also has lots and lots of dolls
Each a model of one of us
It will stick pins in those models
To kill everybody on a crowded bus

Get ready to say your last words
Before you lose an eye or two
Most people say this to their buddies
"I'm done for - I'm going to die too."

Aiko Groves (9)
The Japanese School In London, Acton

Alien Hyena

There's an alien hyena
With dangerously sharp claws
His camouflage is very artful
And, when he laughs, he sends shivers up your
spine
Laughing so loud with blood in his mouth

His favourite colours are black and white
And he really hates to fly a kite
Because he doesn't know how to
He also hates to play with you
If you play with him
Beware, he will bite your face off
With his long, bloody tongue

But if you touch him, he will blush
And take your lungs out
Running deep into the heart of the city
He will hungrily devour your warm lungs
And by then, you will be long gone
So long, goodbye, the alien monster has won.

Kyo Adachi Mavromichalis (9)
The Japanese School In London, Acton

Woll

I am Woll, I have a giant head like a ball
I have a thin but strong body like a chopstick
I love shampoo that smells like bamboo
I also love obedient children
I am friendly, just like a puppy
I have fluffy hair, it was funny
I love all the world's different money
And my dream is to be
The richest monster in the world
I have pretty wings on my back, just like a fly
I hate children who tell me a lie
I can fly to the children who are lying
At midnight, all the children are asleep
I will kill the children who are still lying
From London to China to Timbuktu
If you tell lies, maybe, I'll kill you.

Shizuku Maruta (11)
The Japanese School In London, Acton

Raty Has Appeared!

Raty is in the new zoo
Such a scary monster Raty is -
His gleaming sharp teeth though,
Not scaring the animals one bit.
Raty suddenly appears behind the keeper's bedroom,
And his favourite food is... people!
He runs towards the keeper!

The keeper tries to hide
Raty dashes between them
But the keeper feels happy now - he thinks

Raty bites through the keeper's door
The flimsy door breaks apart
Raty sneaks hurriedly - sneaks in, oh no!
The keeper throws a rock at Raty
Raty freezes up instantly
Raty doesn't like rocks at all
The keeper sighs with relief, safe? Yes!

Hanano Kamabe (10)
The Japanese School In London, Acton

Beware Of The Monster

He appears in a full moon night
He gets energy by eating light
If you don't want to be changed into mice
Don't look at his googly eyes
If he roars
Close your doors
Otherwise, he will eat your soul

When I called the police
I begged them to please
Rush over to assist me because
There's a monster in my house
Trying to kill my spouse

Oh no! Here comes the scary Moon Lion
He is so big and shiny
And the monster is so hairy
Save my dear, dear life
And that of my lovely wife
Perhaps using a big, sharp knife
Will get us out of this strife...

Osuke Ueda (10)
The Japanese School In London, Acton

Killer Tree Comes!

Killer Tree has come
He eats CO2 and people too
Who work at the factory
But he doesn't like dirty CO2
Dirty water and meat
That's simply not his taste
Even though it's a waste

When he jumps in the water
Some slimy things appear
Once you get in that water
You just can't move
Then Killer Tree comes
To eat you or kill you

Killer Tree comes
But he is now quiet
Because he has started farming and fishing
When he is very, very hangry
He will eat small trees
He now works in the factory
And prepares the food that we eat.

Masaharu Sugawara (9)
The Japanese School In London, Acton

The Jhax Monster Comes

It appears after the sunset
Waiting for some bright lights
Flying through the streets
When he sees the shiny light
He goes straight to the site
And eats up all the lights

So people can't read a book
And people can't play in the park
The people can't do any homework
People can't even take a bath

Scary, scary, the Jhax monster is coming
To you with its sharp teeth in view
To take all the lights away from you
Hey, don't forget to switch off your lights
For the light-taker is now in sight
Oh my goodness, he's here!

Tomoharu Sugawara (9)
The Japanese School In London, Acton

Best Monster Dusty

He appears at night
In the clean, clean school
He likes eating dust
Which is his favourite food

He has three googly eyes
To look for the dust
He is invisible at daytime
So nobody knows he even exists

Pop! The dust is gone
But there is more

He cleans all the classrooms
In five, snappy minutes
He has a long, blobby body
Because he eats a lot

He must be the best monster
In the entire universe
He has a rather funny name
Which is Dusty

Pop! The dust is gone
And he is finished...

Julie Marumoto (10)
The Japanese School In London, Acton

Midnight

I opened the door -
Saw blood on the floor...
I went to my room
Trancey the monster was there!
I smashed the door
But going out of the house
There he was - waiting for me!

I quickly called the cops
"Help me!" I begged them
Sadly, they ignored me...
"Sleep, young man, sleep," they shouted.

To get rid of Trancey
Can somebody please help me?
I see him at night -
I see him everywhere -
My body starts to move
Even as I sleep...
Though it's deep in the night...

Ryosuke Kikuchi (10)
The Japanese School In London, Acton

The Great Hydry

The great, great Hydry lives in Driland
With the dry-dry view full with sand
He's walking on the land looking at the sky
Eating the birds that fly really high

"Haw, haw, haw!" the Hydry said
As he strolled around with all of his heads
With all of the birds trying to hide
But before they could, they got eaten and died

And some men tried to hold up their spears
The Hydry looked down and they ran with fear
So if a human is on the boat and goes to Driland
Nobody escapes from the Hydry's hand.

Joseph Duxbury (10)
The Japanese School In London, Acton

The Moonless Night

The moon is out
I hear a creak
The lightning shone and a burst of steam
A glitter of sparkles and a burst of beam
In the moonless night
There sat a bear stuffed with hair
He wears glasses made of grasses
The 10cm bear staring straight up
His jaws ready to eat me
With two or three gulps
A sudden shiver in my body
Brought me up to Heaven to die
A red, glowing liquid squirts in the room
There was that bear sitting so cool

From that day, if he appears
I wouldn't go near him if I were you.

Rikako Saijo (10)
The Japanese School In London, Acton

What Is That...?

When I go to bed, I always hear a grunt
It's not my brother or my dog
I looked under my bed, but there was nothing

I found a blob of slime at the back of my bed
I took it out so I could check it out
When I dropped it, it wiggled and jiggled

I saw it move right before my eyes
This monster is called Grunty
He made a little toy out of gooey slime

He put the slimy toy near me
Then disappeared into the cold, dark night
When I woke up, I thought, *what is that?*

Minori Muramatsu (9)

The Japanese School In London, Acton

My Name Is Buttler

My name is Buttler, I have three eyes
I love to eat children, especially with pies
I have a top hat that's as dark as night
My red eye flashes with dazzling light
My suit is red, it's dyed with blood
I eat any children, they taste very good
I live in your house, but you don't see me
You don't know I'm there until you start screaming
You must be aware of little old me
Or I will kill you and eat you for tea.

Kaede Emma Seki (11)
The Japanese School In London, Acton

Shark Tail The Monster

The huge monster with long fangs
Lives in a shipwreck of ages gone by
Shark Tail his name is
And dangerous he'll always be

He lies in wait for his dinner
Humans and fish his favourite food are
If you swim past his shipwreck
His long tongue will draw you in

Shark Tail is forever hungry
Searching for food is his hobby
Although he is a fearsome monster
He's not always a frightful bother.

Ray Nestor Ito (9)
The Japanese School In London, Acton

I'm Fluff

I am Fluff, I am a monster
I have three big horns, all on my head
I love to eat ice cream relaxing in bed
I have three eyes to find children's lives
I like cutting things up with my razor-sharp knife
I love to play with dice because I am quite nice
But don't ever call me a unicorn
Because, angrily, I will transform into a monster
That's extremely hairy
You could even say I'm exceptionally scary.

Serina Niki (10)

The Japanese School In London, Acton

Midnight Secret

Hi, I'm Lucy, I look beautiful at first sight
But you don't want to see me when the clock hits midnight
I love human blood, especially from a kid
But don't worry, my evil side is carefully hid

I suck their blood and take their life
But when they won't die, my hands are a knife
I chop off their head so that they will die
When it hits the floor, it's time to say bye.

Hinano Aikawa (11)
The Japanese School In London, Acton

Stinkler The Monster

I am Stinkler, I like to wink
I am from the planet Tink
I like to go under your bed
I like to drink your blood that is red

I am huge, green, stinky
I get ill when I kill adults
You will be dead in ten seconds by my stinky gas
It smells like rotten eggs and it comes out of my bum
In the night, I get hungry
You have to go to bed before he comes under your bed.

Kouga Watanabe (10)
The Japanese School In London, Acton

Gloop Da Poop's Revenge!

The stinky monster, Gloop Da Poop, wants to take over
But has nobody to help
He will get a knife and carve 'beware' on a hard brick wall
He has green gloop all over his body
He slurps up children with all the stink
Turns them into live poop
They help him out with all his plans
He is kind of stupid so he doesn't have many helpers
Parents can't see him so, if you tell them they won't believe you
The kids that help him are brown and hairy
They just want to be human again
But Gloop Da Poop says he will kill them if they do, so beware.

Freya Stewart (8)
Thornwood Primary School, Glasgow

The Furry Slumber Monster

He is as creepy as a wolf
Watch out, there's a monster about
His eyes are as green as grass
His big claws scare you at night
His teeth are as dirty as mud
He has two eyes with blood dripping out
Beware, he eats children!
He's the scariest monster in town
Don't go out at night or else you're gone
If you're in bed, don't take a peep
Or else you will be in the old, ugly monster's
tummy.

Stefanie Kokkinaki (8)
Thornwood Primary School, Glasgow

Haunted House

Here is a monster that goes out on Halloween
night
He gives kids a big, loud fright
You hear him scratching at the door
While you tiptoe on the floor
Oh no, can you smell that he is here?
Everyone is filled with fear
I hide under the sheet
While he is saying 'trick or treat'
He's smashing glass around our home
And brushing our dog with a sharp comb.

Watch out people he might come to you...

Anna Marie McShane (8)
Thornwood Primary School, Glasgow

Slimy Bobo Comes To Eat You

S lime in the dark somewhere under your bed
L eft alone, sleeping before he eats you
I am scared of Slimy Bobo
M y heart is scared, shivering, as scared as can be
Y es, this is scary for me

B last, he vanishes in my bed
O h my
"B ut who is that?" said Slimy Bobo
O h no! Slimy Bobo wants to eat me! Help!

Noorhan Al-Wasity (7)
Thornwood Primary School, Glasgow

The Creep Out

He's as scary as a zombie
He's as green as an apple
He's as cuddly as a teddy
He's as slimy as a blob
He's sharper than a knife
He's as evil as a monster
When you see him
He will disappear
Blood will drop down in your brain
He will eat you
You will be creeped out
You will go upstairs
And you will see everything is gone.

Dalia (8)
Thornwood Primary School, Glasgow

The Slow Stealer

As I hear his shooting outside
My fear grows
I know it'll be me next

Bang! Bang! Bang!
My stomach jumps as I hear
The door creak open

Squelch! Squelch! Squelch!
I know it is the Snailmonger
I need to hide my sweets
I've heard myths that he has no mercy
He kills you and steals your trick or treat sweets!

Cal Hanlon (8)
Thornwood Primary School, Glasgow

Platycutiecus

He has a bill like a duck
Watch out or you won't have luck
He lives in a haunted house
Where he would eat children and even a mouse
He has big fangs and scares children with his
monstrous bangs
Comes out on Halloween night causes such a
fright
Crushes everything in sight
Sucks your blood with his scary bite.

Zoë Rowan Detwiler (8)
Thornwood Primary School, Glasgow

Sly Monster

Sly is slick
Sly is smelly
Sly is slimy
Sly is shy

At night, Sly the monster
Comes to you to give you nightmares
Beware, he will write all over your walls
Beware, at night, because he will be there
You will know that Sly has been there
Because your room will smell revolting.

Mabel Elizabeth Gurney (8)
Thornwood Primary School, Glasgow

The Scary Beware

Sharp teeth, short and it's scary
Don't get too close, it will bite
And it will always look in your dream
And it will always creep out of your bed
If you take a little peep, beware
It will crawl out of your bed
And it will bite
That is the end of my story!
Beware...

Ghena Alghamdi (8)
Thornwood Primary School, Glasgow

The Snow Monster

His eyes are as big as an elephant
His mouth is as bloody as a heart
Don't go wandering in the snow monster's cave
Or you will get slime frozen
If you don't go to the cave, you will be saved
A boy called Sam once went through
He got eaten by the snow monster.

Navneet Kaur (8)
Thornwood Primary School, Glasgow

Beware!

Beware!
This spooky monster lurks everywhere.
On Halloween night,
She can eat you in a bite.
But do not fright,
She only comes on Halloween night.
She's as slimy as a slug!
And has the sharpest teeth.
Beware, soon you will be a yummy treat.

Miraaya Sharma (7)
Thornwood Primary School, Glasgow

The Monster

His bloody mouth and hairy, long tongue
Were filled with spikes
He had a vampire body and he never ever smiled
He was always filled with anger
His slimy skin was as green as grass
His vampire body was all purple
He was never good at anything.

Harsimran Sohal Kaur (7)
Thornwood Primary School, Glasgow

Halloween Night

I hear him in my room
Every time under my bed
It is scary, it's an abomination
The scariest of them all
He's coming today
I'd better run and hide
Very scary, gives me the creeps
I hope I will not be next.

Matthew Fletcher (8)
Thornwood Primary School, Glasgow

The Child Snatcher

The legendary monster's name haunts all the
children,
The name of it is Child Snatcher
Its nefarious claws
He can tear down walls with them
That is the end, please beware
The monster is after you.

Eva Sinclair (8)
Thornwood Primary School, Glasgow

Hairy

A long monster that is as green as gloopy slime
As bad as a rat
He likes to go at night to get the children's hair
When they are asleep at night
And eat it in excitement
And go home satisfied.

Nampreet Kaur (8)
Thornwood Primary School, Glasgow

The Booger Monster

This monster bites people in the night
He's green and ugly
He has big feet
He is hairy and hungry
His favourite food is children
He swallows one whole
He eats twenty children a night!

Robbie Sawatzky (7)
Thornwood Primary School, Glasgow

Dash Guy

He came to the party
He sleeps all night and he's scary
Monster is scary in the house
He came right at twelve o'clock
One night, I saw him work and scare
I'd better run away.

Ricky Lin (9)
Thornwood Primary School, Glasgow

Maleficent's Curse

One dark and stormy Halloween night
Maleficent caused a wicked fright
Up and down on the streets
Children walking on their feet
Maleficent hiding in the trees
Cursing everyone she sees.

Aqsa Ahmad (7)
Thornwood Primary School, Glasgow

Spiny Fish

He scratches the walls
When I'm going to sleep
He turns invisible and goes under my sheet
His pointy teeth nibble my feet
Then he goes home to sleep.

Logan Bradley (7)
Thornwood Primary School, Glasgow

The Monsters That Want You

He comes to you at night-time
He wants you
He wants to take you away
He wants your blood
He wants your blood to feed him.

Ibrahim Nazir (8)
Thornwood Primary School, Glasgow

YOUNG WRITERS INFORMATION

We hope you have enjoyed reading this book – and that you will continue to in the coming years.

If you're a young writer who enjoys reading and creative writing, or the parent of an enthusiastic poet or story writer, do visit our website **www.youngwriters.co.uk**. Here you will find free competitions, workshops and games, as well as recommended reads, a poetry glossary and our blog. There's lots to keep budding writers motivated to write!

If you would like to order further copies of this book, or any of our other titles, then please give us a call or order via your online account.

Young Writers
Remus House
Coltsfoot Drive
Peterborough
PE2 9BF
(01733) 890066
info@youngwriters.co.uk

Join in the conversation!
Tips, news, giveaways and much more!

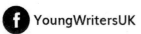 **YoungWritersUK**   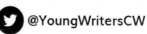 **@YoungWritersCW**